my pet cloud

by Amanda Rawson Hill

illustrated by Laia Arriols

CAPSTONE EDITIONS
a capstone imprint

As an only child, Max had always wanted a pet. His mom, however, claimed to be allergic to mess, noise, and animal hair.

So when Max adopted a lost cloud he found at the park, he thought it would be the perfect pet. Clean, quiet, and no shedding.

Nobody warned him about how hard it is to take care of a cloud.

Okay, maybe his mom tried. But Max was too busy
to pay attention to what his mom was saying.

First, he had to name his cloud. He picked . . .

BROOOM!

Then Max learned how to get Fluffy to thunder-laugh by poking right beneath his anvil top.

HA HA HA!

BROOOM!

From the very beginning, taking care of Fluffy was a natural disaster.

Fluffy ran away at the slightest gust of wind! Max and his mom sometimes had to drive miles and miles to find him.

And Fluffy was almost impossible to house-train.
Nobody could predict when he was going to
precipitate, which led to
A LOT of flash floods
on the carpet.

Then one day, Max and Fluffy were wrestling on the carpet. A shock here, some static there, and ZAP! Fluffy may have started a teeny, tiny fire.

"Nobody warned me that would happen!" Max tried to explain.

His mom moved a rug over the scorch mark in the carpet.

Max and Fluffy decided to prove her wrong.

Fluffy began by showing how helpful he could be.

BROOOM!

He even started earning his keep.

YES!
We are open!

And better than all of that,
Fluffy stuck close to Max—

protecting him
from the sun,

cushioning
his head,

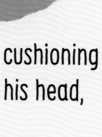

and always being up for
a game of cloud charades.

Max and Fluffy went together like
thunder and lightning. Until . . .

A big storm blew into Max's town without warning.
A rattle here, a boom there, and **OH NO!** Fluffy
was blown away from Max's backyard.

Fluffy pushed against the hurricane-force gales,
but it was no use. He was gone with the wind.

Max and his mom searched the whole next week for Fluffy.
They traversed mountains, deserts, and little beach towns.

They found cirrus clouds, stratus clouds, and plenty of other cumulus clouds. But they didn't find Fluffy.

cirrus

stratus

cumulus

"He might not even be a cloud right now," said Max's mom. "He might be drops in the ocean or humidity in the air. Clouds don't last forever. That's just the water cycle of life."

They ended their search,

but Max kept his eyes on the sky.

Max was so lonely without Fluffy. There was no one to play games with while Mom worked. His pillow was lumpy and uncomfortable. And snow cones made from freezer ice just didn't taste the same.

Worst of all, every time Max went outside and saw the sky, all he could think about was Fluffy.

Then one day, Max was playing baseball.
He was in the outfield when the batter hit
a pop fly. Max ran BACK, BACK, BACK to catch
the ball. He raised his glove in the air,
but the sun was right in his eyes.

All of a sudden, there was Fluffy! He blocked the sun so Max could see. Then Fluffy cushioned his fall when Max caught the ball.

On the walk home, they celebrated.
A spin here, a twirl there, and—

Nobody had warned Max not to get Fluffy
too excited, but they didn't need to.

By now Max was a pro at
taking care of his pet cloud.

Rescue Clouds
Ready for Adoption

Name: Grayson
Cloud Type: stratus
Appearance: low, flat, and blanket-like
Color: dull white to gray
About: Grayson might seem gray and dull, but he is a master of the cover-up. He can hide anything with his fog, which is bad news if you're prone to losing your keys or other important things. But this little guy is helpful too! His drizzle and snow crystals will keep all your indoor plants perfectly watered, and he's nice to have around for Halloween and rock concerts!

*Not suitable for pet owners with poor eyesight.

Name: Chloe
Cloud Type: cirrus
Appearance: stretched thin and wispy
Color: bright white
About: Chloe is the brightest cloud around and brings a smile to everyone's face. When she's near, pleasant weather isn't far behind. This wispy gal deserves an owner who will be around at dusk, as she tends to put on a show at that time and reflects the colors of the setting sun.

*Perfect for people who need a calm and reliable companion.

Name: Puffy
Cloud Type: cumulus
Appearance: big and puffy
Color: white
About: A cousin to Fluffy, Puffy is the quintessential cloud. Kids love her, and she's great for playing Cloud Pictionary. Whenever she's around, you know it's going to be a sunny day.

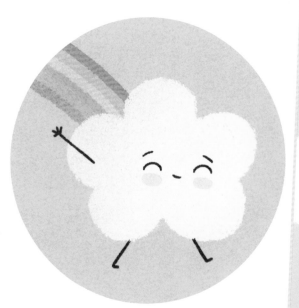

*Puffy must be kept on a strict diet. Feed her too much water and she'll turn into a storm cloud right before your eyes!

3965805

ADOPTED

Name: Fluffy
Cloud Type: cumulus
Appearance: big and puffy

For my mom, who loves all kids and critters.
—A.R.H.

To my mother and sister for their love and support
and my daughters, the reasons why I do this.
—L.A.

Published by Capstone Editions, an imprint of Capstone
1710 Roe Crest Drive
North Mankato, Minnesota 56003
capstonepub.com

Text copyright © 2022 by Amanda Rawson Hill
Illustrations copyright © 2022 by Laia Arriols

Library of Congress Cataloging-in-Publication Data is available on the Library of Congress website.
ISBN: 9781684464258 (hardcover)
ISBN: 9781684464487 (ebook PDF)

Summary: Max brings home a pet cloud, which leads to all kinds of chaos.

Designed by Brann Garvey

Printed and bound in China.   4545